The Puppy's Guide to Training Humans

The Puppy's Guide to Training Humans

All We Need Is Unconditional Love

Cochise with Sequoia

Thornton Reyner Ventures N.V.
PALM CITY, FLORIDA

This book is a work of fiction. Names, characters, places and events are products of the author's imagination or are used fictitiously. Any resemblance to actual events, locations or persons, living or deceased, is purely coincidental. We assume no responsibility for errors, inaccuracies, omissions, or any inconsistency herein.

Front cover and cartoons by Carl Christiansson of Swedish Pictures.

First printing 2005

ISBN 0-9747713-3-3
LCCN 2004101037

ATTENTION CORPORATIONS, UNIVERSITIES, COLLEGES, AND PROFESSIONAL ORGANIZATIONS: Quantity discounts are available on bulk purchases of this book for educational, gift purposes, or as premiums for increasing magazine subscriptions or renewals. Special books or book excerpts can also be created to fit specific needs. For information, please contact Thornton Reyner Ventures N.V., Keith Rhea, 1614 SW Seagull Way, #32898, Palm City, FL 34990; 954-252-2105.

This book is dedicated
to the late primary author, Cochise,
who brought an amazing amount
of love into my life.

It is also dedicated to
Sequoia, Lulu, Grizzly, Buddy, Fifi,
and all those who live in our hearts
and shape our behavior with
unconditional love.

—Keith

Thank you for purchasing this book.
A portion of the profits from
every book sold is placed into a fund
for donations to animal welfare organizations
to help us dogs find humans to love,
and to educate humans on how to care for
and love us, so that we can all live
"a dog's life!"

Table of Contents

Preface

This is a book written by dogs, FOR DOGS. It is a training guide for dogs containing information that has been known throughout the dog community worldwide for many years. Most humans will assume this is a dog training manual in the usual sense, but it is just the opposite. It is the truth behind who trains who. *Sniff, sniff, lick, lick.* As any dog owner, or human companion as we prefer to call them, begrudgingly admits, dogs train people!

Comedian Jerry Seinfeld once said something to the effect that if he visited earth from another planet he would think dogs were the ruling species. After all, where else would one observe humans following dogs around and picking up their poop?

In this guide we will share training techniques and explore from a dog's viewpoint the absurd but accepted human views of dogs. Take dog treats for example: Why are they called "treats"? Sure we sit and roll over when offered a bone-shaped thing with the texture of stale bread but this is not really a treat. We are just happy to have anything other than *dog food.* If a human ate one food every day, every meal, they'd salivate over an earthworm as a change. Does that make it a treat?

At the age of four weeks, I (Cochise) was placed in a home for unwanted pets with my brothers and sisters. Because of this place, I was able to obtain a good human companion and enjoy a long and comfortable dog life. Thus, I will be donating a portion of the profits from this book to various dog-supporting organizations for the continued support of homeless dogs, in the hope that they also find a suitable home.

—*Love without borders or conditions,*

Cochise

Special Note by Sequoia

This book was written almost entirely by Cochise, but was not completed when he went to doggie heaven. I never had the honor of meeting Cochise but through studying and being influenced by his writings I came to love and admire him. He was a special dog, uniquely able to capture the nature of dogs around the world. My role was a humble one, I assembled Cochise's notes, pictures, and other documentation. Cochise's loving human companion, Keith, was very helpful in providing the necessary support to help me get this book to print. As a memorial to Cochise it is dedicated to every dog. It was Cochise's hope that all breeds from all walks of life will have the best of what dog life has to offer them.

Cochise

A Note from Keith

I had Cochise for 14 years as my dog companion and buddy. In his last few years, he lost his eyesight as the result of an operation to remove a tumor. He never stopped giving love and he taught me a lot about this emotion. He holds a special place in my heart. Like humans I have become close with, he will always be inside me even though he is no longer physically present.

I could not simply bury Cochise, so when he passed I had him cremated. His ashes, his collar, and his two favorite squeaky toys are in a container that maintains a position next to my bed.

After he died, I wondered about inviting another dog into my life. Then I remembered the joy Cochise had brought me. So off to the shelter I went with my wife and there was Sequoia, a lab mix similar to Cochise and with a remarkable personality.

As a puppy, Sequoia placed her front legs over people's shoulders and kissed them—and still does today. She benefitted greatly from Cochise's training of us.

I decided to publish Cochise's manuscript to help other dogs with their human companions, and humans with their search for unconditional love.

People—
Picking the
Right One

Humans use the terms "master" or "owner" to designate their role with their dog. This goes back to an ego-stroking need to declare themselves more dominant. Unfortunately, these subservient titles imply "slave" or "property," respectively. Dogs are neither! We are companions for humans, who are companions for us. I like to call them human companions. Isn't that much nicer?

Picking the right human as your companion is a delicate process. A dog must act quickly with a candidate but not make a hasty choice. Primarily, dogs have to be sure the candidate is responsible. Humans should provide care, comfort, love, and *squeaky toys!* Many placement agencies provide assistance with screening. Before I selected my human companion, he had to fill out an application detailing both personal and financial information. He even signed an agreement to have me tutored.

(Or at least that's what I thought. Later I found out it was not tutored but neutered! Ouch! Talk about a miscommunication!)

I have three brothers and two sisters. We were orphaned and placed in a home for unwanted pets in Florida called, of all things, the Humane Society. Philosophically, I found it strange that there had to be a separate organization called this; after all what does this imply about the rest of society? Everywhere should be a humane society and there should be a few remote and secure places labeled "the Inhumane Society" with voluntary and forced memberships available. As John Lennon said, "All we need is love."

At the Humane Society, my siblings and I were placed in a fenced area to be on display for humans to adopt us. I'm not really knocking the place, after all it was better at our young age than resorting to our ancestral roots and hunting for food. Can you imagine? No thanks, that is too much work—and dirty work at that! I rather like the domesticated position we have aspired to over years of evolution.

We were treated quite well there. We received food and water, we played games with the attendants, and we had the company of adult dogs and other puppies.

On the occasion that our gate would open and a prospect would come in to play with us, we had our

•

strategy ready. We held a well-planned be-cute free-for-all. It went like this…when a person came in we would jump and yip, lick their fingers, bite their shoelaces, roll over on our backs to be scratched, jump up on their leg, or any maneuver he or she would think was cute.

The golden rule was not to get too excited, as some times puppies do, and go "wee." Occasionally one of us would get out of our cage and entertain everyone by prancing down the hallway as the attendant chased us. *Sniff, sniff, lick, lick.*

One by one, my brothers and sisters were adopted and carried to their new homes by their human companions. Those of us remaining behind wished them good luck as it was unlikely we would ever see each other again.

After a few weeks, all my brothers and sisters had gone to good homes. And there I remained, mixed in with a few other dogs from other families. I admit I was a high-strung pup. I guess I was too hyperactive for most of the prospects.

One day the attendants came down the hall with several people and some odd-looking equipment. I knew the strange contingent gathered outside my cage were not prospects. As they set up their devices I remember thinking, "Uh oh, has my welcome run out?" I was only six-and-a-half weeks old. My whole life was in front of me. I wasn't going down without a fight. I did my best I'm-a-little-cutie dance; I pawed the gate and licked every finger that came near. With my squeaky puppy voice I yipped for everyone's attention.

I remember the gate opening and someone reaching in to pick me up. I saw a bright light and heard a loud clap, then silence except for a distant deep and serious voice saying, "Between 1985 and today, the number of cats and dogs killed every year has decreased from 17.8 million to 4.6 million, according to the Congress of National College of Veterinarians. That is 8 every minute of every day, largely because they can not find a home. The average age of a dog in a shelter is eight months. There are 15 million stray puppies and kittens born every year. That is over 3,000 births every hour. If you can help give a home to a homeless pet, please contact us."

Then my attendant handed me over to the person who was talking. I licked his finger and continued my playful-and-cute routine. There was more talking and then the light faded. I looked around. The strangers passed me around from one to another. I was being praised, petted, and played with. One of them even had a treat for me to eat!

Heck, I had filmed a commercial! I had just made my TV debut! I was a television personality! I was the King of Cute, the camera's canine, an activist for action! All this attention and I could not remember the last time I had a bath.

The fuss settled down and the equipment was carried away. I was placed back in my cage and given another snack. I thought that with my up-close-and-personal video ad out in front of the entire television-viewing world, it would be only a short time before proper candidates arrived.

Sure enough, that weekend there were more prospects than usual, but I was not interested in any of them—until two days later. A guy came down the hall with the attendant stopping here and there to look at some of the other pups. I played it cool until he was in front of my cage, then went into my routine. He stopped and stuck his finger through the gate. I gave it a sniff, then another sniff pretending to be reserved, then two big licks! *Sniff, sniff, lick, lick.* In that moment, we became drawn to each other. He came in and we paw boxed—he used two fingers and I used my front paws. That was all it took; I was convinced and so was he.

Keith filled out some papers while the attendant put me in, of all things, a cat transport box (demeaning but comfortable). A few minutes later we were in his car and off. I was seven weeks old and being chauffeured into...well...what else, *a dog's life!*

Chapter 2

Housebreaking Your Human Companion

I was out! I had a companion! And soon I arrived at my new home. Keith had a three-bedroom, two-bath ranch home in Florida. The grounds were large and well landscaped and the backyard sat at the edge of prime woodland. We played in the grass and ran around the yard. He fed me premium puppy food and bottled water, and we lolled away the afternoon under a huge covered porch.

The first day was going good, until evening when he put me back in the box, carried it into the garage, dropped in a towel, and left me. I couldn't believe it! He left me in a box! In the garage! By myself! Oh no, this was not going to last long. The very first day in my new home and already I had to start training my human companion. *Sniff, sniff, lick, lick.*

In my best puppy-in-distress voice I spent the next 20 minutes verbalizing my displeasure. I knocked over the box and soon Keith opened the door. I did my I-adore-you-and-I'm-so-cute-you-wouldn't-think-of-leaving-me-in-the-garage-again dance. It worked like a charm.

Keith carried me into the house. But he also brought that darn box and plopped me inside it again. "Slow learner," I thought, but patience is the greatest asset when training a human. I leaned against the side of the box, tipped it over, and I was free again! However, Keith took this as a challenge rather than a reality and he brought in a larger box.

"Oh, how stubborn," I thought, as he set me back in with the food, towel, and water. He must have read in some canine training manual that dogs do not go to the bathroom in the same place where they sleep. Well, whoever came to that brilliant conclusion deserved to have his research grant renewed so that they could record the thought patterns of the brain-dead, in the first person. Who *would* wee where they sleep? Certainly not a dog! In fact, I think humans are the only species in the animal kingdom that do wee where they sleep. That is precisely the reason human babies wear diapers. Yuck!

So there I was in this big box. I was too small to tip it over and Keith was planning to leave me in the kitchen for the night. What do they say about the best-laid plans of mice and men? They often go to the dogs. This was our first night together. I was not about to spend it alone in a cardboard box.

We did a few rounds of me yipping, and him coming in to quiet me, and me yipping again once he left. He finally gave up, carried the box and me into his bedroom, and set me on the floor next to his bed. Now, we were making progress; he was responding very well to training.

It only took a few more minutes of piteous whimpering to make him reach his arm down into the box so I could snuggle up against it. *Sniff, sniff, lick, lick, cuddle.* With that, I figured he had learned enough for one day and we both drifted off to a peaceful sleep.

I spent another week sleeping in that box. Every night Keith hung his arm down for me to fall asleep against. I was growing fast and almost big enough to reach the top of the box. Escape was near! My next tactic was to hook my front paws over the edge of the box and climb by running in place with my rear paws. I was finally successful in tipping the box over and how was I rewarded? I was put back into the garage! Silly human!

There I was, in the garage, a towel spread on the cold cement floor indicating my new sleeping area. This had to change but my yips and pleas were ignored. I think Keith was proceeding on the theory that, "If you go to the child every time it cries it will continue to cry whenever it wants you. Therefore, ignore it. But check in to make sure it is not in any real danger." It was a pity Keith was using such transparent amateur psychology on me. It only got him more deeply enmeshed in a battle of wits that dogs always win.

During the day I was allowed in the house but restricted to the kitchen. I understood this since I was developing bladder control, or as human companions like to say, I was being "housebroken." What does that term mean—housebroken? I suppose that the dog has been broken from the practice of going potty in the house. This is another delusion suffered by humans. Humans think they are training us to hold our number ones and number twos until we go outside. What they don't understand is that when you are only a few months old, controlling these things is not an intellectual decision or a matter of choice. It's a simple matter of physical inability. Might I add that human puppies take a lot longer than we do.

Why are human puppies toilet trained and cats litter box trained but dogs are housebroken? Shouldn't we be yard trained or curb trained? Regardless of the term, as puppies we're just like everyone else; when we got to go, then we got to go.

Well, Keith banished me to the garage at night and when he was away from the house. I figured if I wanted to get back in the house and start lounging on the sofa, I had to gain his confidence by not going to the bathroom in the house. It took me about a month of practice to attain the necessary control. And then, whenever he let me out into the yard, I'd make a big show of weeing on the nearest pine tree (once I figured out that the handrail posts were not good candidates) like I had drunk a tub of water. And then I would proudly trot over to the most plush patch of grass on the whole lawn and do a number two.

This went on for a week and still I was confined to the garage or kitchen. "All right," I thought, "he needs some more training. And he's going to get it."

At this point I was having some serious teething issues, and the drive to chew was paramount. In the garage I figured that I could kill two cats with one stone. The door that led into the house was made of wood, a perfectly grained haunch of wood with a firm but delicate texture and the bouquet of fine oak. I started chewing on the trim, then the exposed corner of the door. Naturally this brought a little discipline my way. I remember his surprise as he yelled, "Cochise, you are eating your way through the door!" I just looked at him and sent the telepathic message with appropriate sad and droopy eye contact: "I only want to be with you."

Eventually, Keith learned that I was determined and finally brought me back into the house before I could chew through the door. As a dog you sometimes have to be a bit extreme to get the human's attention and make your point. Now that I was in the house full-time, I deserved a reward. It was now time to select the piece of furniture that was to become my day bed.

Chapter 3

Furniture Selection

Five days a week Keith went off to work to earn money to pay for our lifestyle, and the house was all mine! This is the time to snooze-test each piece of furniture. I could sleep anywhere—and I did. I never suspected how comfortable it can be to take a nap on something as unlikely as a floral cloth-covered ottoman when the afternoon sun has warmed it up.

We dogs spend a lot of time sleeping—70 percent of our day, in fact. (Puppies sleep 90 percent of their day!) And I like to do so on a bed or sofa. Keith tried to keep me off the furniture, which is typical of early-stage trainees.

In the beginning, I did not let him see me on any furniture. I only left subtle signs such as hair on the sofa or an indentation on a pillow. He knew I was on the furniture but he was unable to do anything, since it would break the primary rule of dog training, which is "catch them in the act."

As he would leave in the morning, I would walk over to the sofa and jump up on it to look out the window. A few times Keith would sneak up on me to see if he could catch me on the sofa or the bed. But he failed to take into account my superior hearing. I can identify Rockports on a mailman from five blocks away, so to me, even in his stocking feet, Keith sounded like a herd of elephants coming down the hallway. I could count his steps and be off the bed and stretched out on the floor half a second before he opened the door. Every time. He could see the indentation of my body on a cushion, but he could never catch me. Sometimes he would walk over and feel the place where I had just been lying and invariably it would still be warm. He'd ask me, "Were you on the bed, Cochise?" and then answer himself, "I know you were, you sneaky dog, and I almost caught you." I'd roll over and try to engage him to play, after all he said my name. (If your name is called, you have to assume it is to play.) *Sniff, sniff, lick, lick.*

Of course, he never caught me. Ever. And that is the prime rule: Do not get caught in the act and your human companion will be unable to do anything. *You can avoid all discipline!* Those silly training manuals say humans must be on the scene at the time the dog is engaging in unwanted behavior,

otherwise discipline is ineffective and counterproductive. So look cute and radiate love, but don't act guilty and don't get caught or it's swats for sure.

Finally, Keith went from trying to catch me on the furniture to trying to prevent me from being on the furniture. He would stand the sofa cushions on edge to make a kind of wall. With a little effort I was able to get them flat or topple them onto the floor. Either way, they were perfect for an afternoon nap. After months, Keith finally learned to leave the cushions alone and simply spread a sheet over them just for me. Persistence always overcomes resistance when training people.

I have heard of some human companions who block off portions of the house by closing doors, installing gates, and using furniture to block hallways. These fortifications are utterly ineffective against the ingenuity of a dog.

Eventually the human rationalizes he or she cannot control you or limit you by simple barriers while they are not home. Once this point is reached, the human has accepted, at least subconsciously, that you are on the furniture when he or she is not home. When that has been established, it is time for the next lesson: *taking open possession of your furniture.*

This requires finesse and infinite aplomb. First, look your human companion gently in the eye as you sit near the piece of furniture you intend to claim. Project the feeling that you wish to sit up on it, but you are not sure you should. Next, rest your chin or a front paw on the piece of furniture to test for any reaction. After a few minutes if there is no response, go for it. One short, self-assured leap and you are there. Curl up quickly, get comfortable, look directly at your human companion, and ooze contentment. I found a deep and slow exhale through the nose was a perfect audible indication that I was comfortable.

If your human companion is a slow learner, he or she may try to chase you off the first few times. But if you have been consistent in applying my principles up to this point, your human will know (at least on a subconscious level) who the boss really is. They will put up only token resistance, enough to keep up appearances and stroke their delicate egos. That piece of furniture—indeed, every piece of furniture— is yours! Enjoy them.

You may even find that your human companion will give you your own special blanket to put on the furniture. Keith used to set up what I call decoy beds. These ranged from a sheet on the floor to a cedar chip beanbag-type thing made for dogs (or so they claim). The intent was to get me comfortable on something other than the furniture. Funny how I never saw him sitting or sleeping on any of these decoys. He would sit on the sofa and try to get me

interested in a sheet fluffed up on the wooden floor. This was not giving me much credit for intelligence.

The final phase of furniture selection is sharing a sofa or bed with your companion and cuddling. Whether you're lying on the sofa with your human watching a movie or just stretched out on the bed at night, cohabitation of the same piece of furniture is the ultimate accomplishment in furniture appropriation. *Sniff, sniff, lick, lick, cuddle.*

It is most easily accomplished with the tried-and-true be-cute-to-get-what-you-want routine. Simply focus your big sweet eyes on your human companion's eyes. Look somewhat upward as this helps simulate humility. Place your paw on his or her arm or leg as if you want to be petted. After a minute or two of this heart-melting behavior, bring your nose to rest on the cushion. When instinct says the time is ripe, place one paw up, wait a moment, then place your other paw up on the cushion. While still maintaining the petting, slowly but with iron determination, inch your chest and stomach up on the cushion or bed. The toughest part of the act is to momentarily appear to struggle. Claw and flail gently with your hind legs once or twice. That is all it will usually take for your human companion to reach out and help you up.

Before anyone realizes what has happened, your back legs will have found their way up and you will be lying comfortably on the couch or bed with your head on your human companion's lap. Reward him or her with your most loving cuddle and you will be home free.

Chapter 4

Housecleaning

As a puppy you have certain advantages a grown dog does not have, such as the teething process. I used this stage to do some housecleaning by chewing up some ratty old sneakers, forcing Keith to get a new pair. I trained him to pick up after himself by chewing to bits anything he left lying around the house.

The exposed wood of old, unsightly furniture is another good choice for some selective teething. This will condition your human companion to keep your house clean and your furnishings up-to-date.

One word of caution, use discretion in what you chew. I do not recommend feminine shoes with Italian labels. I made this mistake once. My defense to Keith was, "I'm a dog. I cannot tell the difference between a rawhide bone and a leather high heel." Keith's defense to his girlfriend was, "It is not the dog's fault; you have to be careful where you leave your shoes."

Neither defense worked. Keith's girlfriend was so upset that he and I ended up in the doghouse for two days, and Keith had to buy a replacement pair of shoes. Hell truly hath no fury like a woman shorn— of her Gucci's, that is! That was some good-tasting leather, though unfortunately she never left her shoes lying around again. She was quickly trained.

Chapter 5

Outside

Although we enjoy the comforts found inside a home, outdoors is a world of adventure and play. All a human companion has to say is "out," and every one of us reacts the same: We do our let's-go-outside dance. Fresh air to breath, squirrels and cats to chase, sticks to chew, trees to pee on, scraps to feast on—the best adventures in life are found *outside!* I admit that on cold or rainy days it does feel good to be cozy and warm, sitting by the fireplace with my head on someone's lap. But normally, *we love being outside!*

Whether you are a city dog limited to concrete sidewalks, small parks, and—I hate to even use the words—"dog runs," or a country dog with miles of grass and woods for your outdoor pleasure, here are some time-tested tricks for extending that all-important outdoor time.

The first rule is to always show interest and enthusiasm for anything remotely connected with going outside. It's easy to make humans feel guilty. If you can make them think they've disappointed you, it might be good for an extra walk. For example, whenever I see someone putting on shoes and/or a coat, I get excited and naturally assume the purpose is to go outside with me. And if I hear car keys jingle I am at the door in an instant waiting to join whoever is leaving, no matter where they might be going. A few pleading glances, a whimper or two, and they think I need to go out.

Once someone decides to take me out, I'm through the door, down the stairs, and doing the happy-body-tail-wiggle all the way. But getting out is only half the battle; the other half is staying out until you're good and ready to come in.

This is when all those lessons on bladder control, learned as a puppy and perfected by constant practice, come into play. The comedian George Carlin did a standup routine in which he explains to his daughter that a dog goes number one and number two. She takes the dog out, comes back, and says it went number eight, meaning four ones and two twos. Don't make the easy mistake of going all at once. Dogs are still hunters at heart and we have to mark our territory. Once you get outside, pee a little but hold on to that number two. If you let it go too early, your human companion will think you are finished and prematurely end your time outside.

Humans know you have to do number two, and they will wait for you. I used to fake it a few times so

Keith thought I was really trying. I would grunt, strain, and look disappointed. Just keep peeing—a little squirt here and a little squirt there. This will extend the outdoor time and accustom the human companion to your need for plenty of time outside. There is a fine line, however. Human companions will eventually lose their patience with all the sniffing, especially if they think you are faking. But we are dogs and that's what we do, we sniff almost everything—including other dogs' butts!

If possible, head directly away from the house and keep on going for as long as you can. Beware of the once-around-the-block walk, which is a circular tour timed to get you back where you started in a few minutes. The first time your human companion tries this on you, hold your business until you finish the lap, let a little pee go and then start sniffing with a focused urgency, moving away from the house all the time. At the very worst this will get your human companion to enlarge the circle. When you feel you have maximized the length of the walk, do number two. Over time your human companion will get used to the fact that number two comes last, and it takes considerable effort to find just the right conditions.

Another method for extending outdoor time is to train your human companion to play your favorite game. Some of us are ball players, some are stick chasers, and some with unusual coordination are even into Frisbee (they are usually showing off for the girl). Don't wait for your human companion to suggest a game; show some initiative. Grab a great stick, drop it right in front of his or her feet, look up, and hang your tongue out and pant while wagging your tail. I guarantee he will throw it a couple times. Sometimes Keith tries to fake me out by only pretending to throw the stick and then watching me run for nothing. All dogs know the joke is on the human. We don't care about sticks; we just want to be outside playing! And besides, there is always a real throw after the fake one. This is a sign that your human companion is enjoying the play. Dogs help humans stay young at heart by having them play. Mission accomplished!

Cats are a wonderful diversion. Dogs know that when we are off leash, we are supposed to stay within sight. But we all have natural instincts that we can't fight. There are cats in every neighborhood. If you pick up the scent, immediately crouch low to the ground. Your human companion will think this is really cute, like we are acting on some kind of primal instinct. Keith called this "sleeping tiger in the grass." Next, launch yourself toward the intended victim. Pretend you do not hear your human screaming, "No!" Then he or she will rationalize your behavior. You were incited—victimized, even— by that snotty cat. The ploy here of course is none of us is interested in cats. They have razor claws and are not any fun to wrestle with, but they are a good excuse for a fast, hard run. Squirrels, or anything else that moves, work just as well.

If you are lucky, you have an athletic human companion and he or she may jog to stay in shape. This type of human loves to run and you love to run. Convince your human companion to take you along; it's a win-win situation. Be careful, though, if your human companion is a serious runner. Those people are crazy. They will go out in all weather and they run much farther then any sane dog would care to go. So if your human companion is not training for a marathon, wait until he or she dons a jogging outfit and sneakers, then stand near the door, wag the old tail, and bark until he or she agrees to take you along. It will become a routine.

These times are great for bonding—just the two of you out in the fresh air. The only negative aspect of this type of trip is that you don't get to stop and sniff as much as you would on a normal walk. This can be overcome by running ahead, sniffing until your human companion catches up, then repeating. This is called the *advance scout routine*. Humans think it is based on an instinct to check out the path ahead for danger. We are scouting all right, not for danger but for good things to smell—and the random edible!

Naturally, real quality outdoor time is spent off the leash. I am a city dog and this is a treat for me. In order to get your human companion to let you off the leash, you must make him or her feel that he or she is still in complete control, even when you are running free. Here are my seven tips for getting off the leash:

1. Never pull—this gives the impression that you need to be restrained; your human companion will pull back.

2. Always prance playfully immediately after being released to show your human companion how much you enjoy the freedom.

3. Stay nearby unless you have an excuse—such as a cat, dog, stick, squirrel, tree, bush, food, person, leaf, or hallucination—on which to blame your lapse in good behavior.

4. Never fight with other dogs, never chase strangers, and never scare children.

5. Never wander too far out of sight, and never stray out of hearing range.

6. Always return, eventually, when called. (You can delay a little by blaming it on poor hearing.)

7. Always show a lot of love. Remember that positive reinforcement is the best way to encourage repeat behavior.

Chapter 6

It's a Nice Place to Visit but We Do Not Want to Live There

Being outside is fun, but it is not where we want to live. Be careful of the extreme human companion who believes we are supposed to be "outdoor animals." This is the human companion who has a doghouse in the backyard and thinks it is just dandy for us to have all that open air and freedom to roam.

Caesar, a friend of mine in Atlanta, has to live like this. His human companion is Mike, an otherwise kind man. He leaves Caesar outside with only a doggie door into the garage. (At least there is shelter if needed.) But Mike also believes in self-feeding doggie dishes and trickle adapters on the water faucet. This means Caesar has to suck his water like a hamster, and he never gets to leverage a long face at mealtime into extra goodies from the table.

In short, Caesar lives like an animal. No doubt

Mike loves Caesar, but this kind of treatment is a natural result of the "outdoor dog" mentality, which you want to avoid at all costs. Caesar, like any of us, would like to be lounging on Mike's king-size bed at night rather than curled up on the ivy in the yard or in his "dog" house. Which brings up the subject of doghouses in general.

Humans believe a doghouse is a good place for us to stay, but when they use the term among themselves, it does not sound so positive. So I looked it up in their dictionary. Doghouse, or more accurately "being in the doghouse," is defined as "a state of disfavor." Why is being in the doghouse good for us but bad for humans? Simple; they never were literally inside one. They use it as a figure of speech, because when they think about it the doghouse is only big enough for us to fit inside. It is usually dirty (no maid service) and the front yard is often muddy or a dirt bowl because of the lack of landscaping. In short, it is a slum shack not a doghouse! There are no windows to look out of, no furniture to lie on. Heck, there isn't even a door for us to close for privacy. Humans don't want to live in a doghouse; how can they expect us to live there?

A doghouse should be defined as "the place where the human companion has decided to live with his or her dog, with soft furniture, comfortable atmosphere, and plenty of toys!"

I have written to the dictionary companies with this recommendation and am still waiting for a reply.

Chapter 7

Inclement Weather

Humans have a strange attitude toward wind, rain, and snow. They act like the weather hurts them. If you want to stay out and play in the rain, special tactics are required. Humans feel that any weather but clear skies and sunshine is an inconvenience. (They have so much to learn from us.) A spontaneous run in the rain rejuvenates the senses. I love wet grass on my paws, splashing in deep puddles, and rolling in the mud. It makes me feel alive and young!

On wet and rainy days it is best to loosen your human companion up a little. You know what has to be done. Right after stepping inside the front door, shake your coat vigorously. It is best to wait until your human companion takes off his or her raincoat so the water shake's effectiveness is maximized.

All human companions know this is coming but somehow it always takes them by surprise. They are cute creatures, though a tad predictable. *Sniff, sniff, lick, lick.*

31

Chapter 8

Food—What Is "Original Flavor"?

Humans have mistakenly adopted the belief (thanks in part to the commercial dog food industry) that a steady diet of the same bland food is a good thing. I have heard pet professionals explain that changing our diet can cause stomach problems, and we certainly should not be given "people" food. Actually, we do have some adverse effects from a change in diet, but this is only due to the excitement caused by the aroma and taste of real food.

Most human companions are afraid of changing our diet because we may have diarrhea. Others consider a change in food the transition from some puppy food, to dog food, to senior food. Or sometimes, your usual brand is out of stock and your human companion is forced into a short-term change. Humans just do not understand the simple truth: Anyone who eats the same thing in the morning, afternoon, and night, day after day, week after week, year after year will welcome a change—even if it is a piece of moldy pizza crust on the floor.

If humans picked their favorite food and had to eat that single food and nothing else, they would not last a week without adding some variety. What is amazing is the shallow thought that goes into what some human companions call variety. Dog treats and dog biscuits, for instance, are usually the same hard food in different shapes and colors. Another great example of a human's idea of variety is alternating wet and dry food and occasionally mixing the two. Well, that is like alternating dry cereal and oatmeal, and occasionally making cement out of the two combined. Yeah, let's call that cuisine extraordinaire! No *lick, lick, sniff, sniff!*

Then there are the "flavored" foods—chicken flavored, beef flavored, liver flavored, beef and cheese flavored, and my favorite, original flavor. What is *original* flavor? It is not the taste of raw flesh; it is the first taste the dog food company decided to manufacture. This begs the following question: Who did the taste testing at the manufacturing plant? I have never heard of a taste-test panel of dogs. Have you ever seen a sample platter person in the dog food aisle at the grocery store offering samples on toothpicks to dogs passing by to get their feedback? Nope, never! So who is doing the decision making?

The operative word with all this food is "flavored." It is nothing but the same junk with a different flavor and color. It is not chicken; it is the same old dog food flavored to taste like chicken. I bet humans never even read the ingredients on those cans as they do with their own food.

This required a little investigation. I rounded up a few cans of food to review the ingredients...*yuck!* I would rather eat my furry squeaky toy than what is in that can pretending to be dog food! Let me share with the rest of you dogs what the humans are trying to feed us. I will not disclose the brand but it is safe to say that most brands use the same general ingredients, which sound like what is swept off the floor of some disgusting factory.

> Chunky, with Beef. Ingredients: water, meat by-product, chicken, beef, soy flour, poultry by-product, sodium, tripolyphosphate, potassium chloride, carrageenan, locust bean gum, salt, natural flavor, guar gum, caramel color..."

The rest is a bunch of chemicals and vitamin additives. What are "meat by-product" and "poultry by-product"? Back to the human dictionary: By-product is defined as "something produced in addition to the principal product, a secondary and sometimes unexpected or unintended result." Maybe this is where the "chunky" comes from? When I pawed through the dictionary to look up the word "meat," I actually found the full term "meat by-product." Ready? Well, hold onto your stomach! The definition is "a usable product other than flesh obtained from slaughtered animals." *Puuuuuuuuke!*

Let me continue to the final analysis.

Every dog should also be aware of the fat content of food. The same can of food I described above has the following breakdown:

- Crude protein—minimum 9.0 percent

- Crude fat—minimum 5.0 percent (Looking good so far—low fat!)

- Crude fiber—maximum 1.5 percent

- Moisture—maximum 78.0 percent

- Calcium—minimum 0.22 percent

I know I am a dog, but I was not aware moisture was one of the four basic food groups. And what exactly is *crude?* Back to the dictionary (It's a good thing I can read!). Crude is defined as "existing in a natural state and unaltered by cooking or processing." In other words, *raw protein, fat, and fiber!*

That clears it up! This particular dog food is raw undefined animal chunks from the slaughter process! No way I am eating this stuff even if my human companion eats it first. The scraps in the garbage can are looking rather appetizing in comparison.

Here is the best line on the entire can of "Chunky, With Beef":

> Animal feeding tests using AAFCO procedures
> substantiate that (brand name) Chunky, with
> Beef provides complete and balanced nutrition
> for the growth and maintenance of dogs.

This required a little web research (It's a good thing I know how to use a computer!). I typed AAFCO into the search engine and sure enough, up pops "Association of American Feed Control Officials." I looked through its board of directors and members, and just as I suspected there was not one dog listed. I will concede that the organization has a somewhat reasonable purpose: "The basic goal of AAFCO is to provide a mechanism for developing and implementing uniform and equitable laws, regulations, standards and enforcement policies for regulating the manufacture, distribution and sale of animal feeds; resulting in safe, effective, and useful feeds."

No mention there about tasty! Could you imagine human food being described as "safe, effective, and useful"?

Then there are the other types: "Chunky, with Beef, Bacon, and Cheese" and the "Prime Cuts in

Gravy with Chicken and Rice. In addition to the ingredients listed in "Chunky, with Beef," there was "cheese meal" in the "Chunky, with Beef, Bacon, and Cheese" and "animal plasma" in the "Prime Cuts." I am not even interested in looking up those terms in the dictionary.

But in my search for AAFCO, I found a few other listings that interested me. I'll share them here, so those dogs without Internet access can be fully informed.

First there is the list of AAFCO dog food definitions, which listed

> meat by-products—the non-rendered, clean parts, other than meat, derived from slaughtered mammals. It includes, but is not limited to, lungs, spleen, kidneys, brain, livers, blood, bone, partially defatted low-temperature fatty tissue and stomachs and intestines freed of their contents. It does not include hair, horns, teeth and hooves.

Only a few of the other terms on the dog food cans were listed there, which I suppose means the company can make up their own definitions.

The next thing that was interesting was the AAFCO dog food testing procedures. For adult maintenance dog food to pass the AAFCO test, the following must be true:

- Eight dogs older than one year must start the test.

- At start all dogs must be normal weight and health.

- A blood test is to be taken from each dog at the start and finish of the test.

- For six months, the dogs used must eat only the food being tested.

- The dogs finishing the test must not lose more than 15 percent of their body weight.

- During the test, none of the dogs used is to die or be removed because of nutritional causes.

- Six of the eight dogs starting must finish the test.

That's all there is to it!

I am not saying all commercial food is like this. During the last 10 years I have noted premium and gourmet, *human quality* food for us being put on the market, which is a better choice of evils. But basically, using a little human irony, all this stuff is *dog* food! This is no way to live.

We are natural carnivores, after all. Thousands of years ago we lived in the wild and hunted our own food. Not that we want to go that route anymore, but a juicy steak with some gravy, a good slice of veal, or some leftover chicken is always welcome. Brothers and sisters, I know you have dreams about good food the way I do. Let's explore sources of enriching your diet.

I conducted a survey that concluded 70 percent of the humans requesting a doggie bag at the end of the meal for their leftovers are going to eat the food themselves, 15 percent intend to eat it themselves but leave it at the restaurant, and 10 percent intend to eat it themselves but end up throwing it out. That means 95 percent of all doggie bags are not going to the doggie! Hello-o-o! Something is wrong here!

Through some historical research, I have been able to detect that the origin of the "doggie bag" was started by a Victorian upper-class woman who was too embarrassed to say she wanted her leftovers to take home and eat herself. So she quietly asked the waiter to place the remains in a bag for her foo-foo poodle. That poodle saw none of it! *Webster's New Collegiate Dictionary* defines "doggie bag" as "the presumption that such leftovers are intended for a pet dog; a bag used for carrying home leftover food and especially meat from a meal eaten at a restaurant." The key word is "presumption."

So how do we do it? How do we get a more robust menu to choose from? I've picked up many techniques for adding more flavorful items to my cuisine. A source of great variation is those unexpected finds on the streets and sidewalks discovered during routine walks. The key here is to spot the item without letting my companion know the reason for the diversion. I casually sniff in a certain direction and as soon as I'm within snatching distance I wolf down the gourmet item. *Sniff, sniff, lick, gulp!* Usually it's a piece of bread or cookie dropped by children. If I'm really lucky and am having a good day I can feast on pizza crust or restaurant leftovers.

Of course after I've eaten I have to hear the same old speech: "Cochise, stop eating garbage," or "You're such a trash hound." Well, obviously, if I had some variety in my diet I wouldn't have to stoop to eating off the street. Please look at the stuff I was being fed every single meal. *Yuuuuuck!* Human companions do not understand that if we ate like they do we would not have to eat scraps off the ground.

The key to unlock this dilemma is that most human companions believe that human food is not good for us. Hey come on, most human food is not good for humans. I am not interested in a hotdog, or some other processed mush that is only differentiated from dog food by its shape and marketing. I am talking about a nice piece of beef, chicken fillet, occasional pasta, and my favorite—bread in any form. How can human companions believe this is not good for us? We were originally carnivores that hunted down other animals before we decided to tame humans to be our companions.

"Don't give dogs scraps from the table because they will get used to it and beg" is another ignorant statement. Let's look at this piece by piece. "Don't give the dog scraps." I agree, don't give me scraps either—I expect a full portion of my own. This is the same line of thought that leads to "Don't give dogs chicken bones because they can choke on them." Very true, this is no myth. But who in their right mind eats chicken bones? Take the meat off the bone and give it to me, or make my day with a boneless chicken breast. We do not like to eat bones. But we are so grateful for the ability to eat something that we will gnaw at the bones to get as much of the taste as possible. Sometimes in our excitement we chew a bone to splinters. But, I digress.

Let's look at the rest of the line: "from the table." Most books human companions read on dog training state that if we are fed from the table we will associate the food with the table and will be prone to begging there. These books suggest giving scraps, to the dog well after the meal has been completed. Who do they think they are dealing with? We do not care *when* we get the food; we only care *if* we get the food. I strongly recommend locating yourself near the table in a quiet but obvious manner as a reminder to save some food. Also, if you hang out during the cooking process, the human companion may just prepare a little too much or give you a sample.

The last part of the line is "because they will get used to it and beg." Oh, come on! We should not have to *beg!* We should not be given the same food over and over again! What is wrong with getting used to eating a variety of food? Plus, we are not begging, we are training. Begging is just another dominant human term to support their frail egos. We are educating the human companion that it would be far more noble of them to feed us some variety. Begging is to plead to others for something they have and you need. This is not what we are doing. We are not pleading; we are increasing our human companion's awareness.

One of the things I used to do that worked great was to not eat my bowl of food until Keith finished his meal and cleaned up. First of all, during mealtime I was sending my hungry glance at him trying to obtain whatever scrap I could. But the great guilt move is that once the meal was done, I would walk over to my bowls, and lap some water to cleanse my palate and prepare the digestive tract for the hard, flavored nuggets. I would eat my whole bowl. Eventually, Keith realized that I only eat after he does and would place leftovers on top of my bowl of nuggets. Occasionally, a little gravy or tomato sauce would be ladled over my food. Slowly, gestures like these were made routine and my diet improved.

Occasionally, I would eat only the leftovers, pausing for a few minutes while looking around for more. Staring at my human companion, I'd lick my chops and slowly go back and eat the nuggets. This little interlude is a great guilt builder and occasionally is good for more leftovers that were destined for the refrigerator.

Chapter 9

Attention Antics and Tactics

It is especially good to use a squeaky toy to get attention. When I squeak a toy, no matter how upset my human companion may be, he always smiles.

Many of us feel that our human companions do not spend enough time with us. We are social creatures and we often like to be the center of attention. Granted, we sleep around 70 percent of the time, but when we are awake we want to play. Sometimes we have to get our human companion's attention by barking, sniffing, licking, pawing, staring, standing, hugging, gassing, or "bed runs."

Barking is the most common attention-getting move we have. It is age old, but in the right circumstances still very effective. Sophisticated barking at the right moment can be just what you need to redirect your human companion's focus. There are three basic types of barks: (1) the half bark, or woof, (2) the multiple bark, and (3) the yip.

The most effective bark is the half bark, also called a "woof," followed by a series of tail wagging and prancing. The woof sound is made by muffling a full bark, that is, by closing the mouth halfway through the bark, which lowers the volume and exclamatory nature of a full bark.

Repetitive barks become annoying, not to mention hard on the vocal cords, and should be used only in extreme situations. I don't like barking for too long. What will the neighbors think? Usually if you bark too long, human companions think they need to ignore you and you will stop, or they feel there is something wrong and you need their help. The irony of this second angle is that the human capacity to understand what is wrong is fairly limited. For example, I was chained to a tree in the backyard on several occasions. How barbaric! After about 15 minutes of solid barking, Keith came out to see what was the matter. He went back in after thinking nothing was wrong (his opinion only). So I had to bark for five minutes more before he returned. "Nothing wrong?" I thought to myself. Nothing except this chain connecting me to a tree! What would happen in an emergency? What if a cat came by and saw me? I would lose all self-respect and be the object of feline mockery. After a while, Keith finally improved his behavior and let me loose.

Yipping is the higher-pitched bark typical of small dogs. Yipping is very annoying and quite effective in making the human companion completely unable to focus on anything else. Like barking, yipping is fine for extreme situations.

The main thing to keep in mind when barking is not to "cry wolf." This means that you should not bark unless you have a good reason, otherwise people will stop paying attention to you when you do bark. I might suggest an update to this cliche, which is, "Don't cry, just woof." This means do not whimper about a situation; just give a cute woof to get some attention.

Of course, there are many other ways to effectively gain attention other than barking. I would often just follow Keith around the house or outside. Wherever he went, I went. Sometimes he would stop short and I would walk into him. How cute can I be?

When he would settle in somewhere, I would settle in nearby. When he got up and started walking, I got up and started following. After all, he could be going to the bedroom where I could lie on the bed, or the kitchen for food, or out the door. I was not going to miss anything.

Sniffing and using your nose is good also for attention. I used to tap and tip things with my nose to indicate I wanted something. I would open almost-shut doors using my nose as a wedge, and sniff at the door when I heard Keith coming home. He would hear me as he unlocked the door, knowing his greeting committee—me—was excited to see him. And you can use your nose to leave cute reminders of yourself, such as nose prints on the window of your home or car.

Licking is good—real good. *Sniff, sniff, lick, lick.* I can sometimes lick a hand or thigh for 10 minutes or more. No one can withstand that. The humans think this is because we need salt, but it is simply our way of being affectionate and getting some attention.

Pawing a leg or an arm and pulling it toward you is good, too. Be careful not to have muddy paws or to leave a mark on the good clothing of your human companion.

Staring. Ah, staring. Nothing can be more heartwarming than the direct long stare of big brown dog eyes. Occasionally, Keith would lie on the sofa and watch a movie or read a book. After following him to the room, I would settle in with a long audible exhale. Then I would position my head to rest on both my front paws and lock eyes on Keith. Every time he looked at me, I was staring at him. Sometimes we would get into staring contests. But eventually, he would melt and would think I was too cute, and he'd ask me to jump up on the sofa with him and cuddle. Mission accomplished!

I would also combine staring with a squeaky toy. Stare while squeezing the toy to make its sound and you are practically guaranteed attention. Or try holding the toy or your leash and staring. This is also very powerful—bound to put a smile on the human's face and affection in his or her heart.

Standing, particularly the rear-leg stand, is usually reserved for small dogs, such as Jack Russell terriers or poodles. Heck, some poodles would act as though they went to ballet classes the way they could get around on their hind paws. I was never very good at this, but Twix, a golden retriever, was great at it, especially for his size.

The full-body hug is good for medium to large dogs, but works just as well for small dogs, although it is more of a full-leg hug. It is not recommended for the giant breeds, such as Great Danes. A friend of mine, Otto, who happens to be a Great Dane, stood up and placed his paws on his human companion's shoulders one day and started to lick his face. The human companion fell backward from the weight, while Otto stayed on top of him, still licking. Otto nearly suffocated him!

Gassing, also know as the silent gas bomb, is not the most preferred when it comes to attention techniques. Sometimes it can backfire if you just had a recent change of food. The silent gas bomb is that no-noise-eye-watering-make-people-leave-the-room fart that we can let out with little or no sound. Do not expect anyone to come right on over and pet you but you may get let outside immediately. Another friend of mine, Trouble, (how is that for a name?), used to go to the office with his human companion and sleep in a room where four or five guys were working. While sleeping Trouble would send out a silent gas bomb, which was good for at least three mentions of his name in the office as well as the suggestion that he be let outside.

Bed runs are good when you have "nonmorning" human companions. You know the type I'm talking about. They sleep in, slowly become conscious, and then take their time getting out of bed. This situation is easily remedied with a frenzy of activity.

[Note: I, Sequoia, would start at one end of the apartment, a toy in my mouth, and run through the living room, through the office, past the bathroom, down the hall, and with a single leap from the bedroom door threshold land on the bed. What great fun! I would promptly prance around the bed like a queen, stepping over and sometimes on my human companion, showing off my toy. Using this technique, I was able to train my human companion to get up at 6 A.M. every day to take me out for a walk. Then after the walk, I could eat and relax, while he tried to sneak a few more minutes of sleep.]

There are endless cute things we can do for attention because we are the Kings—and Queens—of Cute and always ready for love and play!

Chapter 10

Embarrassing Moments and Other Observations About Humans

All I can say is, "Thank goodness I am not a poodle." No offense, really. Some of my best friends are poodles. But I couldn't imagine being paraded outside in one of those tight little sweaters, my hair shaved into shapes meant only for bushes, and brightly colored bows tied all over my body. This isn't cute, believe me. And other dogs are laughing hard and thanking the gods above they don't have to be subjected to this type of humiliation. We dogs don't wear clothes and we hate going to the doggy salon. Humans should take that money and buy us treats and toys!

But we all have our share of embarrassing moments and experiences we would rather forget. I will try to give you some hints on how to combat humiliation with humor.

53

Regarding those outfits: Poodles aren't the only ones who suffer. Let's consider the holidays. Yes, that time of year when you are expected to put on stuffed reindeer antlers or a Santa hat, or wear a big red bow around your neck and pose with the family for the annual card. (My poor friend Ralph in Minnesota has human companions who live for those holiday cards and take pleasure in coming up with outrageous ideas. One year they harnessed him to a Santa sleigh that was pulling their one-year-old baby.)

My advice—be a good sport. Put up with the slight humiliation and have some fun. You are loved and can indulge a little silly behavior from time to time. When you have had enough, simply roll around on the ground until the stuff comes off.

Chapter 11

Significant (Human) Others

On my list of human companion characteristics, the single guy rates high, but—and this is a big *but*—along with the male human companion comes *the girlfriend*. Don't get me wrong, girlfriends can be great. The smart ones realize that most guys are secretly thinking "love me, love my dog" and they will do anything to win you over. They can actually be your biggest ally and will often feed you from the table, invite you onto the couch or bed, and welcome you to come along basically anywhere.

Whatever you do, however, *do not chew her shoes*. Forget that she left them on the floor and they look like another leather chewy treat. *Never* chew her shoes! (It's amazing a girl could have so many shoes and get upset over a few teething marks in one lone shoe.)

Significant others are definitely good to help you get on the furniture and for other things such as food. Over the years, I've found that significant others are effective allies. They just can't resist me when I sit at their feet and follow their hand with my big brown eyes as the food goes from plate to mouth.

I don't know how many ventriloquist stunts I've pulled by getting a significant other to speak for me: "Keith, Cochise wants some of the pasta. Can he have some bread? Do you give Cochise the leftovers?" The power of dog telepathy!

Chapter 12

Monday, Saturday— What Is the Difference?

Humans have a funny way of labeling their days. One day is called Monday. This is the day they are usually tired and not in a good mood. The next day is Tuesday followed by Wednesday, Thursday, then Friday. Friday is usually when human companions tend to relax. The day after that is Saturday. This is the day my human companion sleeps late. There is no alarm clock. There is no morning rush to leave the house and he hangs out all day doing what he likes.

The same thing occurs the following day, which is called Sunday. Together Saturday and Sunday are called the weekend. This is important for us dogs to remember because human companions act differently based upon the day. Ah, dog life. For us, every day is like their Saturday.

I have tried to get my human companion to treat every day like Saturday, but it has not worked. (Even I do not have all the answers to human companion training.) My observation is that it takes many dog lives to get a human companion to understand every day is Saturday. But by then they are not as active as they used to be in their younger days. In fact, the funny thing is that humans call this time "being re-tired." When finally every day is Saturday, they are tired again. What fun is that?

Chapter 13

Words

Look up "dog" in the dictionary and here are some of the definitions you might find: "a worthless person," "something inferior of its kind," "ruin (go to the dogs)," "an investment not worth its price," "a slow-moving or undesirable piece of merchandise," "an unattractive person," "a theatrical or musical flop." . This is insulting! Do the editors think we don't read?

If you would like to help eliminate the negative definitions associated with being a dog, write to Webster's and tell them that you, as a dog, are insulted by the negative connotations the English language has placed on being a dog. Insist that dictionaries help correct the situation by not reinforcing it through their publications. The definition of a dog should be, "a carefree, intelligent, fun mammal capable of radiating unconditional love."

Other notable words in the human language are as follows:

- Doggie bag—a way for a human to transport table scraps usually not intended for the dog

- Doggone—damn (two words, doggone, funny isn't it?)

- Dogma—life according to dogs

- Dogged—stubbornly determined

- Dog-day afternoon—other than a great classic movie, it also describes being fully relaxed in the midday sun on your favorite piece of furniture

- Dog-tired—how we feel after a day without our usual 16 hours of sleep

- Dog breath—comes from eating the same food for years and not brushing our teeth

- Dog's life—what humans want to live if they did not have to work to support us

  And let's not forget d-o-g spelled backwards.

Chapter 14

Outdoor Sports

Just when things were getting really comfortable for me in my old age, my human companion decided to buy a sailboat. You might think this is wonderful. Sailing out on the open water, wind, sun, new people to play with....Not necessarily.

I must admit, the first time they invited me I was thrilled. You know the moves. First it's the hyper jumping around, then the tail wagging, and the tongue hanging out—the whole yeah-I-want-to-get-out-of-the-house routine. Then it's in the car and to the dock. Freedom at last. But hold on. What's this bright orange thing being strapped around my body. A life jacket? I don't think so! How am I supposed to look cool with this goofy thing on?

Of course, I soon realized that without it, I would have to do the doggie paddle for quite some distance to get to dry land. And it served as an excellent body pillow. It really wasn't so bad once I thought it over.

For those of you who don't sail, let me tell you from a dog's perspective it's no hike in the woods. First, I have to step off the ground to a wobbly dock, then onto a boat that moves around even more. Finally, I find a place to wedge myself on board and we leave the dock. Okay, this is nice...cool breeze blowing, sun shining, and all's right with the world.

But just when I get comfortable we change directions in a flash, and I go sliding to the other side of the boat, water splashing everywhere. And there are no soft couches here. We're talking fiberglass and plastic seats with a flotation cushion for a little softness. I thought I might stay in the Yacht Clubhouse next time with that cute little dog on the boat across the dock.

Hiking and camping. Now these are activities my human companion should do more of. I can't think of a better way to spend my weekend. First it's the car ride to the park. Then it's days filled with activities dogs like best—walking in the woods freely with no annoying leash, chasing squirrels to my heart's content, scouting ahead to keep my group on track (no need for those little markers on the trees, I can follow any trail by scent), and then nights spent under the stars. (Well, I really slept in a tent, and I do prefer a soft bed or couch to the ground, but we can't have everything.)

My human companion has this thing about responsibility and for some reason he thinks that I should carry my own food and water. And some smart son of a gun happens to have invented a doggy backpack. Very cute! I figured that if I was going to be invited back, I should not complain about having to haul a little of my own gear.

Chapter 15

Learning and Lessons

I found in life that a lesson often leads to more learning. An answer to a question generates another question. So what I have attempted to organize here is a beginning.

The relationship we have with our human companions is a dear one. While we train them to adapt to living with us, they also bring us great companionship. They watch over us.

Humans live longer than us dogs. When we leave them we want to leave them with a feeling of love, appreciation, and the desire to have another dog companion. We know the next puppy our human companion will have is not a comparison to us, but a continuation of the unconditional love in their life. And remember, the next puppy will appreciate *your* training when they are automatically placed next to the bed in a box as a puppy, given the free run of the yard, or held while napping. *Sniff, sniff, lick, lick, cuddle!*

Unconditional love is all we need.

Good Human Companion Characteristics

I do not claim to be an expert, but here are some points to keep in mind when selecting a human companion. This list is the result of extensive research by a brilliant dog named Manny, who is a chocolate lab and a longtime friend. The full study can be obtained from the Psychology Association for Dogs under the title "Candidate Characteristics and the Pre-Determination of Good Human Companions Versus Bad Human Companions."

Responsible

The root of this word is "response able." Dogs need to be taken care of. We need lots of love. We need a human who is able to respond to our love.

Dog person

Never go with a cat person. A cat person trying out a dog in his or her life is not good. We don't do tryouts. A cat-and-dog person is too unstable. They are unable to fully commit and you'll be subject to comments such as "We can leave the cat for the weekend, but what are we going to do with the dog?" A dog person is the only way to go. See if there is a history of dog/human companionship and check references.

Morning person or night person

Whether you like to get up early in the morning or prefer to sleep late, you're going to want a companion with similar preferences. I am a morning dog and often I have to wake my companion up to get my morning walk. That is bad enough, but he doesn't just wake up and take me out right away. Instead, he wakes up, shuffles around the house, gets a glass of water, takes a shower, gets dressed, makes coffee, eats... Get the picture? And worst of all, then he goes to the bathroom. And I'm standing there, busting my bladder! Can you believe that? Hello? Calling the shelter for abused animals! Why does he get to go to the bathroom? Because he can't hold it! Meanwhile, I have all four legs crossed and my eyes are starting to roll back into my head.

Active

You want someone who is about as active as you are. If you are hyper get a hyper companion, if you are sedate get a couch potato. A pairing of opposites is going to be uncomfortable for both of you. I remember an Irish setter named Scotty who never sat down. He would run around the house with his toys begging his companion to play with him, but the only time the guy even responded was when Scotty got into the line of sight between him and the TV. At times I think Scotty wondered if TV was a rival for the title of man's best friend.

Available time for having fun

It is a published statistic that puppies sleep 90 percent of the time and adult dogs sleep 70 percent of the time. So when my companion gets home, I am ready to play! He may be tired but I do the welcome-home-I-missed-you-let's-play-and-run-around-after-I-lick-your-face happy dance. *Sniff, sniff, lick, lick!* This is the 30 percent of my life when I am awake. Let's have fun!

Affectionate

The nice thing about being a dog is that we can cause most adult humans to act like children. They talk funny to us. Heck, just the fact that they talk to us is funny. Then they use a silly voice and the whole thing gets hilarious. It's cute and endearing. I recommend that you find a companion who talks to you in that funny way. It's a good sign that their inner child is alive and well.

Playful (aka Full of Play)

The fountain of youth is defined in dog lore as playing with toys. You want someone who will buy you toys for entertainment, both yours and theirs. I have a small collection of rubber squeaky toys, which includes Mr. Frog, a hamburger, Ms. Bear, and couple of furry squeaky dolls. These are great; I like to pretend that I am sending a Morse Code message to my companion by picking one up and randomly squeaking it while looking him right in the eyes. This always puts a smile on his face, no matter what mood he is in. (Where is Pavlov during these moments?)

Human Companion Candidate Stereotypes to Avoid

The this-one-we-will-train-right candidate

These humans always come on strong with the latest fad in dog obedience training. They are convinced they are intellectually superior to dogs. Max is a German shepherd friend of mine. His companions, Norm and Penelope, simply refuse to accept their place in the relationship. Max and I listen to them talking about "being an alpha" and "making sure the dog knows who is the boss" and on and on they go. He humors them when they need it. Poor Max has had a slow time training but progress is being made. It would be so much simpler if Norm and Penelope, and all humans, would just admit that *dogs rule!*

The we-want-a-dog-before-having-kids candidate

Be careful of newly married couples if they are using you as a surrogate baby. You will receive lavish attention until they think they are ready to have a puppy of their own—human puppy, that is. Stock up on your toys early and be prepared to share them with the human puppy. And in return you may be able to play with the human puppy's toys. Just don't eat or bury them.

The let's-get-a-dog-to-teach-our-child-responsibility candidate

You see, dogs are supposed to be the carefree ones! To match us up with a carefree human child is either going to be a lot of fun or chaos. If it turns out to be chaos, the dog should suggest the parents buy a goldfish for the kid and hire a dog walker.

The I-will-impulsively-get-a-dog candidate

How many Dalmatians found homes because of that movie? How many of them found that when the novelty wore off, the attention and affection also evaporated? Do not select a companion who looks at you as a novelty. The sure sign of this intent is if they try to put a bow on your head and give you as a gift, à la Fifi la Poodle.

And of course there are the instant candidate rejects, such as when they :

- Show up with a chain leash and spike collar big enough to anchor a boat.

- Arrive in a white surgical gown mumbling to themselves, especially if their name is Dogtor Frankenstein.

- Wear camouflage and talk about hunting. This means you may have to work for a living and will probably be kept outside and treated like an animal.

- Are concerned about your "papers." This may mean they are thinking of you as an investment. You could end up on the show circuit. Don't get me wrong; it is not a bad life but it is hard work. And what happens when you pass your prime? Ask any five-year-old greyhound about this. You should not be asked to prance and perform tricks for a panel of judges, retrieve dead birds, or be forced into gambling institutions. You're a dog. *Dogs rule*, therefore, *we do not work*.

Acceptance Techniques

Once you have the right candidate you need to close the deal. Here are seven tips for catching a prospect's eye and instantly securing a place in his or her heart:

1. Be alert for new prospects. If you see them first you will have the edge in getting their attention.

2. Get their attention! Dance, yip, paw, jump, quiver, act cute—do whatever it takes to get them to come to you. Do the I'm-so-cute dance.

3. Be as clean smelling as possible.

4. Look them in the eye. Dogtor Barney has concluded that humans can fall in love with a dog after only 30 seconds of uninterrupted eye contact.

5. Give them as many dog kisses as you can. Remember *sniff, sniff, lick, lick.*

6. Play with anything they give you.

7. Try not to get so excited that you go wee.

Sometimes, we dogs are faced with having to turn away a bad prospect. The best methods are to act lethargic and sickly or play dead. A little bow-wow-barf on their shoes means goodbye for sure.

Simple Dog Wisdom to Live By

- Nap daily.

- Play daily.

- Nap again daily.

- Do the happy dance when you are happy.

- Be consistent and you will get what you want.

- Licks are better than barks.

- Treat every day like Saturday.

- Remember who feeds you.

- Don't settle for original flavor.

- Spread as much fun and love as possible, without borders or conditions.

If you have funny stories or pictures
about your human companion or tips on how to
train your human, please send them to us at
Thorne@TRVentures.com

or mail them to Keith Rhea,
1614 SW Seagull Way, #32898,
Palm City, FL 34990.

Give the Gift of

The Puppy's Guide to Training Humans

to Your Friends and Colleagues

CHECK YOUR LEADING BOOKSTORE OR ORDER HERE

❑ **YES**, I want _____ copies of *The Puppy's Guide to Training Humans* at $12.95 each, plus $4.95 shipping per book (Ohio residents please add 81¢ sales tax per book). Canadian orders must be accompanied by a postal money order in U.S. funds. Allow 15 days for delivery.

My check or money order for $_____ is enclosed.

Please charge my: ❑ Visa   ❑ MasterCard
                  ❑ Discover   ❑ American Express

Name _____

Organization _____

Address _____

City/State/Zip _____

Phone_____ E-mail _____

Card #_____

Exp. Date_____ Signature _____

Please make your check payable and return to:

BookMasters, Inc.
P.O. Box 388 • Ashland, OH 44805

Call your credit card order to: 800-247-6553

Fax: 419-281-6883 • Email: order@bookmasters.com
www.atlasbooks.com